Samuel French Acting Edition

I0586971

Seven Santas

by Jeff Goode

SAMUELFRENCH.COM   SAMUELFRENCH.CO.UK

FOR PRODUCTION ENQUIRIES

UNITED STATES AND CANADA
Info@SamuelFrench.com
1-866-598-8449

UNITED KINGDOM AND EUROPE
Plays@SamuelFrench.co.uk
020-7255-4302

Each title is subject to availability from Samuel French, depending upon country of performance. Please be aware that *SEVEN SANTAS* may not be licensed by Samuel French in your territory. Professional and amateur producers should contact the nearest Samuel French office or licensing partner to verify availability.

MUSIC USE NOTE

IMPORTANT BILLING AND CREDIT REQUIREMENTS

Dedicated to

Arthur Aulisi
Jessica Davis-Irons
Andhow! Theater Company (New York)

Chris Covics
Unknown Theater (Los Angeles)

Emily Joy Weiner
Houses on the Moon Theater Company (New York)

Dale Gregory
Rogue Theatrics (Los Angeles)

for believing in this play
before
it was written

Thank you.

SEVEN SANTAS was developed through a series of productions, which premiered November 25 - December 7, 2007:

Bailiwick Repertory
(Chicago, Illinois)

Directed by Robert Bouwman

RED	Ted Jonas
KLAUS	Jason Goedken
SAINT	Linda Rudy
NIQ	Matt Rudy
KRINGLE	Benjamin Haile
J.O.E.	Sara Kay Snider
BIG S	Michelle Renee Thompson
MRS. CLAUS	Deborah Smith
Assistant Director	Miquela A. Cruz
Stage Manager	Robert Pitts
Costume Designer	Kitty Mortland
Lighting Designer	Logan Finley

Ensemble Productions
(Minneapolis, Minnesota)

Directed by Grif Sadow

RED	M. Scott Taulman
KLAUS	Kevin McLaughlin
SAINT	Mark Benzel
NIQ	Matthew Glover
KRINGLE	Bryan Grosso
J.O.E.	Jim Bitney
BIG S	David Schlosser
MRS. CLAUS	Peggy Endres
Producer	Jan Peterson
Set Designer	Jeffrey Mosser
Costumer	Kat Pepmiller
Sound Designer	Lowell Prescott
Dramaturg	Melanie Spewock
Stage Manager	Jeffrey Mosser
Graphic Designer	Jesse Ross

Open Fist Theatre Company
(Los Angeles, California)

Directed by Darin Anthony

RED . . . . .Michael Patrick McGill

KLAUS . . . . .Frank Ensenberger

SAINT . . . . Michelle Lema

NIQ . . . . .Tisha Terrasini Banker

KRINGLE . . . . .Bjørn Johnson

J.O.E. . . . . Rodney Lee Sell

BIG S . . . . Chris Erric Maddox

MRS. CLAUS . . . . Samantha Bennett

Produced by Martha Demson

Assistant Director . . . . Adam Kinsinger

Costume Design . . . . .Sherry Linnell

Scenic Design . . . . Donna Marquet

Lighting Design . . . . Dan Weingarten

Sound Design . . . . Peter Carlstedt

Prop Master . . . . Daryl Dickerson

Postcard Art . . . . .Jesse Ross

Graphic Design . . . . Maia Rosenfeld Photography

Publicity . . . . David Elzer, Demand PR

Stage Manager . . . . Katie Cadle

Board Operators . . . . Rebecca Rosenak
Sarah Buster

Running Crew . . . . Bill Elder

Chico Cabaret
(Chico, California)

Directed by Jeff Dickenson

RED	Quentin St. George
KLAUS	Paul Stout
SAINT	Allen Lunde
NIQ	Jerry Miller
KRINGLE	Don Eggert
J.O.E.	Mike Clemens
BIG S	Jeff Dickenson
MRS. CLAUS	Judy Clemens
Assistant Director	Stephanie Adams
Costume Designer	Donna Foster
Lighting Designer	Dinah Russell
Stage Manager	Dinah Russell
Light & Sound Op.	Dinah Russell
Poster Art	Jeff Dickenson

Renaissance Theatre
(Huntsville, Alabama)

Directed by Criss Ashwell
Assisted by Tanja Miller

RED	Wayne Miller
KLAUS	Todd Hess
SAINT	Jeremy Woods
NIQ	Mel White
KRINGLE	Tom Voight
J.O.E.	Tanja Miller
BIG S	Daniel Yearta
MRS. CLAUS	Mandy Hughes

PRODUCTION NOTES

SEVEN SANTAS runs approximately 80-90 minutes, which may be the appropriate length for a one-act play in some communities, and a bit long in others. If you need to add an intermission to the play for your production, it can be inserted at the beginning of Mrs. Claus's monologue, by having her declare a 'smoke break', and then reconvening for the second act, as follows: *(Insertions in italics.)*

MRS. CLAUS. I think Santa needs a rest.

Thank you for that share, hon, that was endearing.

Let's get you some coffee. Decaf.

No, it's okay, you sit down.

Somebody help him.

Okay, wow. I could use a cigarette after that.

Back in ten. Fifteen, if I find my hip flask.

Vilmer, get back here!!

[INTERMISSION]

[ACT TWO…]

All right.

Is there anybody else?

Vilmer, did you want to say something? Then shut up!

SANTA 1 – "RED"
"I'm not gonna say it"

I'm not gonna say it.
I know I'm supposed to.
I know that's what you expect.
But too bad! Coal for you. You're not gonna get it.
That's where I draw the line.

I know my rights. And being silent is one of 'em.
Which is appropriate, since it's Christmas.
I also happen to be holy and bright.
Bright enough to know:
You say the wrong thing at the wrong time—one time—in
   public, on the record—And that's it.
You never get that genie back in the bottle.
That's all anybody thinks about you after that.

How many kids have been branded as "bedwetters-for-life"
   off of one thing their little brother shouldn't have said
   on the playground at recess?
How many elves have been tarred as acorn smugglers—
   Even though they never found those goddamn
   acorns!

All it takes is one slip of the tongue, and you got your foot
   in your mouth.
Next thing you know, there's rumors going around you got
   a boot fetish—when you don't even like the taste of
   leather!

(**MRS.C** *'S not what I heard.*)

So you gotta watch what you say.
And you don't even have to say a word: 'Cause it could be
   anything.
You could be sittin' there, mindin' your own business.

Tryin' to eat a cookie.

Somebody tells a joke, you laugh. You shoot milk out your nose.

You're coughing, you're choking, you can't get your breath—You could sure use a Heimlich, but they're all too busy laughing their ass off to help!—You're gasping and shaking like a bowlful of jelly—And now it's too late.

That's all anyone remembers from that Christmas party.

"Hey, you remember that time you almost swallowed your tonsils?"

Yeah, I was the one spent New Year's in the I.C.U., asshole.

"Could you do it again? That was hilarious!"

Now you're the guy who gorges on cookies, and shakes when he laughs like a total buffoon. It doesn't matter how many toys you deliver after that.

You'll always be the slob with the gingerbread fixation and the spastic laugh.

Who also happens to deliver toys.

How do you think that feels?

To be jolly and fat no matter how much weight I lose.

Or lively and quick, even when my arthritis flares up.

To be thought of as merry and gay long after the definition has changed.

People expect me to be jovial 24/7. Like a fucking child.

I'm a grown man.

I've got ideas about politics.

Does anybody want to hear them? No!

"Just sit in the chair and chuckle for the kiddies, fatto."

I could solve the Middle East right now. Does anybody want that?

(**MRS.C.** *No!*)

Give me six thousand in small bills and a sleigh full of dreidels, and I'll have this whole thing wrapped up by Hanukah.

"Forget it, flabby. Just do the bowlful of jelly and bring us a PlayStation, Lego set, Barbie dolls, makeup, and an iPod. ...Oh, and world peace." Mother fuckers.

How'd I get saddled with a stupid laugh, anyway?
Why did that stick?
I never laugh.
You fly over the whole world once a year, and take a look down.
    Tell me if anything's funny after that.
People need Prozac after some of the shit I've seen.

But I'm not supposed to talk about that.
That's not what you expect outta ol' Saint Nick now.
You'd rather hear me repeat what's already been said so
    many times, so many ways, it doesn't even mean any-
    thing anymore.
                    (**MRS.C.** *Quit stalling.*)
It's just a simple phrase. What does it matter if I say it?
You've already decided what you're gonna believe or not.
But if I don't do it, I'm in denial. Or I'm trying to hide
    something. And I look like even more of a liar—or a
    cheat, or a prick—or whatever else you wanna make
    me out to be this week.

Nothing I say makes me look good,
and saying nothing makes me look worse.
                    (**MRS.C.** *Then shut up and say it.*)
Fine. I'll say it. Will that make your season bright?
That's why we're here, after all.
I'll give you what you want. 'Cause that's what I do.
That's the kinda guy I am.
So let's do this and get it over with:
You probably don't want to be sitting on my lap for this.

Hi, my name is Santa.
...And I'm an alcoholic.

SANTA 2 – KLAUS
"Supply and Demand"

What is addiction, really?

It's supply and demand. That's all.

Your body wants something. Or your mind.

Or your, y'know, down under parts.

And you either supply that need – or don't supply it – based on whether the demand for the same is strong enough.

And if you tend to want the same things over and over,

you tend to satisfy those needs in the same way. So a pattern forms.

That's not really an addiction.

A habit, maybe.

But there's nothing magical or sinister about it.

And people kick habits all the time. Why?

Because the desire to continue the habit ceased to be stronger than the desire to refrain therefrom. It's that simple.

It's no mythic battle of Man versus Id.

It's not an obsession.

It's just supply and demand.

The only reason anyone has an addiction to *anything* is we haven't given them a good enough reason not to.

Honestly, we wouldn't have addictions at all if the non-addicts didn't need them to make their own proclivities seem kosher and customary.

You never see a smoker horrified that another smoker can put that crap into their lungs.

It's only the non-smokers.

> (**MRS.C.** *Sure, blame the victim.*)

Alcohol didn't used to be an addiction, either.

Because everyone understood:
You're thirsty. You're Irish. It's Friday.
We get it.

And it's not just substances that are abusive.
Now there's gambling sprees, and shopping binges. Work-
    ahol.

> (**MRS.C.** *Sex-ahol.*)

Videogames... internet porn...

> (**RED.** *What's wrong with sex-ahol?*)
> (**MRS.C.** *Hey, make mine a double!*)

How did these get to be addictions?
Quite simply, because *you*, the consumer, need them to
    be.
So you can pat yourself on the back for not having them.
Or put it on the insurance if you do.

And that's how it works. The world, I mean.
What do people want – need – demand? And can you
    supply that?
And if the answer is "yes". Then you're in business.
And if the answer is "no".
You're in philanthropy.

How do I provide toys to a planet full of children at no
    cost to them and still turn a profit? Very simple: Chil-
    dren – want – toys.
There is no greater and more unrelenting demand in the
    galaxy.
Adults want things, too. But not all the time. And not
    consistently.

> (**MRS.C.** *Sex-ahol.*)

But a child always wants a toy:
Constant and unlimited demand.
And supply?
Just one night.
365 days in a year: Only one Christmas.
And what happens when you take the most irresistible
    economic force in the Universe—a child's love of

playthings—and squeeze it through a hole 365 sizes too small?

You get a laser beam.

Any physicist will tell you: Shove enough photons through a pinhole you get a flashlight that'll punch through solid steel.

Now multiply that by four billion children worldwide, and you've got an economic engine that generates a revenue stream of almost pure profit.

It's simple Reaganomics:

The real money is on the supply side.

The kids are a loss leader—something you give away free to get the parents in the door.

Department stores can write off a GameStation, if they sell Daddy an entire home entertainment system on the way out of the toy section.

So now they pay me to give the stuff away.

They have to.

Imagine what would happen if I stopped delivering toys:

The global economy would collapse.

> (**RED.** *Who died and made you Pope?*)

You think I'm kidding? Look at the numbers:

Retailers operate in the red the entire fiscal year until Black Friday—the the first day of Christmas shopping.

Because Christmas means toys.

And toys have accessories.

And accessories have tie-ins, and tie-ins have product placement.

And you pull the wrong Jenga and the whole thing comes crashing down like a house of dominoes.

Think about the movie industry, for instance:

Where would they be without holiday films?

And I'm not just talking your traditional 'So-and-So Saves Christmas'.

You've also got your 'Hanukah Hijinks with the Humorsteins', and the latest Kwanzaa hip hop-umentary—or a Ramadan spy caper—all coming out in the Yuletide frame. Why?

Because any religion that wants to stay competitive in this
  market has to slot a holiday in December so their kids
  don't get greedy and convert to Christmas-ism.
So now "holiday" films are a tentpole of the industry.
And you know what happens to the Christmas tree when
  you can't find the pole:
The whole thing goes back in the attic until next year.
And just like that, the motion picture industry goes under.
And the television industry goes with it.
Because without movies, where are you gonna get has-been
  actors to star in your sitcoms?
And then the fast food business!
Because who's gonna eat a happy meal if they can't get the
  latest Pixar toy in it.
And without the food service industry, where are you
  gonna get the supporting cast for your sitcoms?

(**MRS.C.** *How 'bout Canada?*)

Canada! And then the terrorists win!

Or look at the airlines:
They're hangin' on by a tinsel as it is, waiting for that holi-
  day uptick.
But what kid wants to visit wrinkly old Grandma in winter,
  if they're not going to get a toy out of it? She's got the
  thermostat set on 58, and the place smells like Vapo-
  Rub.
And no parent is gonna get on a crowded plane with two
  and a half pissed-off brats to visit the in-laws in Podunk,
  if there's not some kind of kickback on the back end.
So air travel plummets.
Rental cars, hotel bookings, turkey farming, decorations,
  wrapping paper—And most importantly: Presents.
I don't mean toys.
I'm talking big ticket items:
A washer for Mom, a power tool for Dad, a fur coat for
  Dad's girlfriend.
'Cause how're you gonna buy your spouse that nice neck
  massager she's always wanted—and/or electric ball
  washer he really needs—if you got the kids sitting

there staring at you with that "what about me" pout on
their little faces?

So they all stay home – they stay in – they eat leftovers.
And they tell the kids that Christmas
is just an ancient religious cult the Romans used to feed
the lions.

Can you imagine?
If people found out this was a religious holiday,
that would be the end of Christmas-as-we-know-it.

SANTA 3 – SAINT NICHOLAS
"The Miracle of the Persimmons"

That's all it was when I was a kid. An obscure religious observance, that I half-suspected my father made up to get a three-day Sabbath.

Once a year, Poppa would light a candle in the window and say a prayer to the Heavenly Father who sent us his only documented son to sacrifice himself for our salvation. And then he'd sit us on his lap and read us the entire Book of Matthew. Then he'd wake us up and sends us upstairs to bed.

And after he tucked us in, he'd sit by the window the rest of the night, puffing on an old stump of a pipe he held tight in his teeth. Staring into that candle.

I used to think the candle was baby Jesus—who is the light of the world—but as I got older, I realized it was the star that shone down upon Bethlehem town. Poppa wasn't commemorating the birth of our Lord and Savior. He was simulating the ancient star that lured the Wise Men from the Orient bearing gifts of gold, frankincense and myrrh. Especially the gold. He had big plans for that gold.

You see, Poppa was a cobbler. At a time when cobbling was not the rage. People were starting to take their shoes "no cobbles". Plus there were a couple of lady cobblers who were taking a lot of his business.

      (KLAUS. *Supply and demand.)*

He thought about taking them to court and having them burned as witches, but he couldn't afford the legal fees. In those days, you needed a chicken just for a retainer.

So Poppa prayed for gold. Not that he was greedy, or vindictive. But to him gold meant a new life. A chance to get out of a dead end-business and maybe open a blacksmithy. Become a tinker, or a wainwright. Something with a future. And that's what Christmas was to him: A golden opportunity. One magical day that could turn his whole life around.

But the other families in the village were devout pagans, and they just laughed at us. "You think your magic candle will bring you gifts? Ho ho ho! Come! Forget your foolish superstitions and celebrate the real and tangible feasts the Goddess of Winter has prepared for us. This year she's making pumpkin pie!"

They were a jolly, festive lot, the pagans. And they would celebrate anything: Eclipses, solar flares, colorful tides. Unusual birthmarks, obscure harvests. Tree bark that looked like someone's face.

When a pig was born, they'd celebrate with bonfires and cinnamon apples.
When a pig died, they'd celebrate with ham sandwiches, and bacon-wrapped cinnamon apples.

One time, I snuck out of the house and went down to the village square, during the fall bacchanal, just to see what it was like.

It was wonderful...

They were celebrating Oaktoberfest: the first Tuesday, after the first Monday after the oak leaves turned whatever color they happen to turn that coincides with the arrival of the first beer sleds from the North. There was plum pudding and mince pie for everyone and candied acorns and wreathes of mistletoe. And beer and spiced rum, and hockey and caroling and all the things we never had at Christmas.

And for the adults, there were colorful red and green tents that people would go in two-at-a-time and come out with blissful holiday smiles on their faces. And sometimes three-at-a-time. I'd never seen anything like it. I could have stayed there forever.

But it was past my suppertime. So I stole a pocketful of acorns and smuggled them home to share with my brothers and sisters.

When my father found out, he was furious. He didn't believe in taking things from other people's gods. The Bible said, "Do unto others as you would have them do unto you." And he had no intention of sharing his frankincense with anyone else when the Wise Men finally came to town.

But I was furious, too. "Why can't our holidays be like that?" I yelled across the table at him, "Why can't we be happy just for once?!"

[shrugs] I was just a kid.

He never spoke about it again. But I knew I had disappointed him.

So the pagans partied and we stayed home with nothing. And Poppa sobbed into his candle, year after year, wondering why the Holy Magi had abandoned him again.

So one Christmastide, I gathered up all the scraps from the floor of my father's shop, and sewed them together and made a boot. And sold it to a man with one leg. And used the money to buy persimmons from a withered old Greek man who owned a nearby orchard.

That night, while my father slept, I placed the persimmons on the windowsill next to his candle. When he awoke the next morning, and saw that his prayers had been answered, he rushed out into the street and shouted for all the neighbors to come and see what the Orient Kings had brought him.

(**MRS.C.** *Christmas persimmons!*)

It was like a miracle. Because suddenly Christmas was real. Somehow, that simple childish act of kindness had turned all his fables and white lies into reality.

Poppa strutted around the front yard with his persimmons, and everyone marveled at him and praised him for having faith in such a stupid faith.

All except the orchard owner. He was a despicable old man. And when he saw what I had done, he came to my father and said: "Your son Niklos! Your son Niklos! It is no miracle. Your son Niklos brings persimmons." But the old man's accent was terribly thick.

(**RED.** *Your son Niklos! Your son Niklos!*)

And instead of "son Niklos", they thought he said "Santa Claus".

(**KLAUS.** *Yer Sani-Klos! Yer Sani-Klos!*)

And "presents" instead of persimmons. So the villagers— who liked that explanation a lot better than the idea that my father had been blessed with his own personal miracle—all leapt up and cried: "Yes! Yes! Santa Claus brings presents. He does it every year. To celebrate the winter solstice! Come, let us bake a fruitcake in his name!"

(**RED.** *Y'know, I still have that fruitcake.*)

It's funny we don't associate persimmons with Christmas. Because that's how it all started.

(**MRS.C.** *Funny, ha ha?*)

(**RED.** *Or funny, fucked up?*)

And every year after that, the orchard owner secretly sent me a bushel of persimmons to crush my father's faith with. But I left them on the windowsill anyway, or on the mantle, or in old socks he'd hung by the chimney to dry. Because I knew that the Christmas gifts did *not* crush his faith. My father knew in his heart it was not Santa Claus bringing persimmons, but the Holy Spirit. Or baby Jesus. Or the Magi.

(**MRS.C.** *Virgin Mary?*)

And sometimes he thought it was the Virgin Mary. Or
father Joseph. Or shoemaker elves.

...But he never suspected it was me.

SANTA 4 – NiQ
"The Secret is Elves"

And that's when it hit me—Elves!

That was the answer.

> (**MRS.C.** *What was the question?*)

I didn't know the question. But I knew the answer was
elves.

> (**RED.** *Idiot.*)

Because in those days, everybody had elves.

Every shoemaker, anyway.

It was the only way to keep up with the workload.

During the week, you took in shoes, cobbled as many as
you could—then on the weekend, the elves came in
and finished the rest.

And elves are workaholics.

The harder the job, the happier they are to do it. You don't
even have to pay them.

Overwork an elf long enough, and they'll pay you.

So it occurred to me that if I came up with an assignment
tough enough—impossible enough—I could get elves
to work for me for free forever.

> (**KLAUS.** *Now we use Asian children.*)

My father's shop had two elves, Vilmer and Freddik.

I sat them down and I said: "Picture this:

A new toy for every child at Christmas. Are you in?"

Vilmer said "yes", right away.

In fact, he thought he could get some of the neighbor
elves to go in with us. Every elf in town was going to
want a piece of this!

But Freddik—he's the cagey one—he says: "Hold on:

Every child in the village? Or every child in the whole
valley?"

That's when I knew I had him.

"Every child in the *world*," I said,
"And we do it... Every year."
His eyes lit up like lights on what would one day be called
    a Christmas tree.
"And we deliver them... All in one day."
"That's impossible!" he shrieked, and fainted dead away.
And the next morning I had every elf in the village knock-
    ing at my door.
And the day after that I had every elf in Europe.
And the day after that...
Well, I knew we had to move.

We were going to need to dig a secret underground bunker
    in a remote forest somewhere, so the elves could work
    in privacy.
But elves are notoriously poor diggers. Small fingers. We
    lost an entire year scratching around in the woods.
And as winter set in, the ground got even harder. Digging
    was slower.
And then it started to snow. That's when it hit me!
                         (SAINT. *Double pneumonia?)*
Snow! Anyone can dig in snow.
All we had to do was move the whole operation north:
    Build on a snowfield. It was brilliant!
And the timing was perfect: Property values at the North
    Pole had hit rock bottom. I bought the entire ice cap
    for a handful of beads and a song.
Unfortunately, the song was "Jingle Bells".
Today, those Eskimos are billionaires.

So we moved everybody north—built a snow village—and
    we got to work making toys.
But no sooner did production get underway, than we
    started losing elves right and left.
Literally, losing them.
Little tiny elves in little white parkas? Impossible to keep
    track of.
We're still turning up corpses, every time they plow the
    main road.

Whenever elves went to the outhouse, half of them didn't make it back. Why they always had to go in pairs, I'll never understand.

Then one day, I was out watching elves urinate into a snow-bank—And it hit me!

(**RED.** *Faceful of blowback?*)

Colors! No more whites. Rainbow colors! Yellows, browns and pinks. Harder to lose in the snow. And easier to keep clean.

I started having Mrs. Claus color-code everything: Green for the elves, blue for condoms, silver and gold for presents.

And me: Red fur, head to toe.

(**KLAUS.** *Red's a power color.*)

With a little white trim, to show I care.

But the biggest problem, living practically at the North Pole—was that we lived practically at the North Pole! What was I thinking?

Before long, we had an entire shipment of toys ready to go and no way to get them there!

We were going to need huge wagons with snowshoes for tires. Or an abominable snowmonster with a gigantic backpack. Or a whole army of sled dogs...

And then it hit me!

(**SAINT.** *Enough with the hitting.*)

What animal do we have plenty of in the arctic? That's immune to inclement weather and strong enough to pull a sleigh?

Answer: Polar bears.

Flying polar bears!

With flying polar bears, you could deliver anywhere in the world.

And bears are strong so they can pull bigger loads, make fewer trips.

And nobody's gonna mess with you.

I mean, seriously, if you see a giant polar bear parked out-side next to a bright red sled, are you gonna mess with that shipment?

Not if you like your fingers.

(RED. No shit.)

So we captured some polar bears—taught them to fly—
   and that Christmas, we loaded up and hit the skies.

What a sight!

I still remember the look on those children's faces the very
   first year when I soared into town with a sleigh full of
   toys and eight giant polar bears.

Terror. Sheer terror.

I told them not to panic, but they wouldn't listen. Children
   ran screaming away with their gifts. Too frightened to
   be grateful.

In town after town, the story was the same...

And then my lead polar bear—Randolph—mauled a
   child.

(RED. Oh!)

And in the next village he mauled another one.

(SAINT. Jesus...)

By the time we reached the third village, word had spread:
   Santa Claus was coming to town.

(MRS.C. Better watch out.)

The villagers met us at the gate with torches and pitch-
   forks.

But an angry mob is no match for eight highly-trained
   flying polar bears—who had acquired a taste for
   human blood.

It was a massacre.

I don't know how many villagers died that night.

I don't know, because we never did find all the parts.

But I counted at least 26 arms and 12 legs.

And I lost one of the bears.

Randolph took a pitchfork in the femoral. He wasn't going
   to survive. I had to finish him off myself.

If you've never strangled a bear—in the middle of a mob
   riot—I don't recommend it. It gets pretty ugly.

The screaming and roaring—blood and flames everywhere—and then... Snap!

(MRS.C. ...Oh shit.)

[silence]

That could have been the end of Christmas as we know it.

I stood there shivering in the silent night, covered in
　　gore—Thank God the suit is red—thinking: What the
　　hell was I thinking?!
It really tested my faith.
And the elves.
Not the polar bears so much. They were fine. They were
　　ready to go again.
But it definitely shook me up.

But I remembered my poor father, when times were at
　　their worst—calmly sitting by the window staring out
　　at the new-fallen snow. Patiently puffing on that old
　　stump of a pipe.
And I realized that no matter what went wrong—or how
　　bad things got, or how stressful—smoking would
　　always get me through it.
I might have to bump it up a pack or two, during shipping
　　season—but tobacco would always be there for me.
　　　　　　　　　　　　　　(**SAINT.** *God bless it.*)
And I wasn't going to let the death of dozens of innocent
　　parents stop me from doing what I had to do:
Bring Christmas joy to the children
...of those massacred parents.

SANTA 5 – KRIS KRINGLE
"Children are all I care about"

To tell the truth, I guess the children are all I really cared
about.

> (**SAINT.** *Suffer little children to come unto me.*)

The love of children is the purest kind of love.

Bringing joy to a child is a pleasure most people never
experience.

Sure, they love their own children, maybe. Or they say they
do.

But do they make them happy? Truly happy?

> (**MRS.C.** *Define happy.*)

Let's face it, caring for one's own child is a legal, moral,
ethical and genetic obligation. And where's the fun in
that?

But to bring a smile to the face of a child you've never
met—A total stranger at the shopping mall sitting on
your lap and telling you all the things in the world that
could brighten their Christmas morning—and knowing you can do that for them...

I still get goose bumps.

That's a truer affection than some will ever know.

A child who gets a present from me doesn't care about my
weight or how I look.

Or if my beard is too scratchy.

They love me for me. And my toys. And vice versa.

And part of them always will.

Even if they eventually grow up and stop believing in some
of the things we did to celebrate Christmas.

That's why I like elves.

They never lose their childlike wonder and enthusiasm,
and outfits.

I got my passion for children from the elves.

When I was younger, working in my father's shop, I used to wake up early every Saturday to watch the elves coming in to work.

And sometimes they'd let me come with them!

We'd take our leathers into the backroom of my father's shop. And Vilmer and Freddik would sit on my lap. And we'd cobble the day away.

It's a custom in elven culture for the shortest to sit on the lap of the tallest, so naturally, I always had an elf or two perched on my knee, beaming up at me. Yammering excitedly about ribbons and bows and mistletoe.

It was like working with excitable, precocious, magical six-year-olds with adorable lisps. Half the time, I couldn't even understand what they were saying.

I'd get so lost in the twinkles of excitement dancing in their child-like eyes.

They could talk about choo-choos and sweetmeats and sugar plums for hours and hours. And I would listen.

And then we'd grab a hot tub.

There was a natural hot spring near the village that the elves had converted to a private spa.

                       (**KLAUS.** *Very resourceful.*)

They're *very* resourceful, the elves.

And they have the cleanest pores you've ever seen.

One Saturday afternoon, Freddik was mixing margaritas, and I was helping Vilmer salt the rims, and it struck me how much he looked like little Frannie Raufvensh-emmer, who lived a few streets over and down the hill at the Kindersklavenlager Orphanage.

And also took very good care of her skin.

Frannie was a shy girl.

Who never spoke to strangers.

Or even looked them in the eye.

But if you brought her a present, she would come down to the gate and talk to you.

And then you weren't a stranger anymore.

But one day, the nuns caught her playing barber with some
of the village boys.

They didn't actually catch her, but she kept coming home
with lollipops she couldn't explain.

After that, they didn't let her go out to the gate anymore.

I would walk by and see her standing at the window of the
orphanage, staring out at the snow. Like my father.

Only sadder. Because she still had so much life in her.

It made me wish someone could get in there, and let her
know she wasn't alone.

And she hadn't been forgotten.

Well, the orphanage had an unusually large fireplace.

So one night, while the nuns were asleep, I jimmied the
gate, and climbed up onto the roof.

But I made such a clatter that the nuns all ran out onto the
lawn to see what was wrong.

And while they were distracted, I shimmied down the wide
chimney, and crept up to Frannie's room.

I must have been quite a sight.

Standing in the doorway—my face covered in ashes and
soot. Coughing and choking in spite of myself.

I tried to laugh it off, but I probably looked like some kind
of monster.

Frannie didn't stop screaming until I reached into my
pocket and pulled out a lollipop.

Then she recognized me.

And she smiled...

She said, "Kris, is that you?"

So maybe she recognized the lollipops.

I didn't care. That smile was what I came for.

The smile of a child is the most beautiful thing in the
world.

You try it some time:

Go to the candy shop in the mall and buy a fist full of
candy canes and give them to the first little girl or boy
who sits on your lap. And see if their laughter doesn't
make you feel like heaven.

(**SAINT.** *For heaven's sake.*)

Or maybe that's bad advice.

I guess you shouldn't give candy to strangers.

Or presents.

Or tell them your name is Kris when it's not.

But Frannie didn't seem to mind.

She made me realize that Christmas shouldn't just be about lifting the spirits of grumpy grownups like my father.

She showed me that children are the ones who really know how to appreciate presents.

It's in their eyes, and their smiles, and their little hands.

Frannie didn't even have to say "thank you" to show you how grateful she could be.

And I enjoyed making her grateful.

Even if technically it was breaking and entering.

I guess that's the difference between a good deed and a crime:

Do you feel good about it afterwards? Or dirty?

(**MRS.C.** *Or both.*)

Eventually, I stopped feeling dirty.

And that's when I knew it was okay to give presents to children.

At least I wasn't killing their parents.

SANTA 6 – JOLLY OLD ELF (J.O.E.)
"The Country That (Coulda) Killed Christmas"

[laughing] HO HO HO HO HO! So I switched to reindeer
the next year. And whole thing started coming together.
The elves got along well with the deer. And children aren't
afraid of reindeer, the way they are of bears.

(**MRS.C.** *Except for Jeannie Rancini.*)
(**RED.** *I don't wanna talk about that.*)

A child can walk right up to a deer and pat it on the nose
and it won't tear their arm out of its socket. And deer are
natural flyers. Not like polar bears, who have to practice.

In fact, there were so many flying deer in those days, we
used to have trouble going into rural communities, because
all the local reindeer would fly up to meet us, if one of the
does was in heat.

I started carrying gingerbread cookies to distract the wild
bucks. Mrs. Claus baked them for me. When we ran into
a stag swarm, I'd throw a handful of cookies over the star-
board side and while they were diving down to catch 'em,
we'd veer left and come in for a landing.

The Industrial Revolution took care of the deer problem.
Something in the air.

(**KLAUS.** *It's called "profit".*)

Now you rarely see deer flying in the wild. And it happened quick, too. One year, smoke coming off the factories
was thick enough to navigate by. Very next year. No flying
reindeer.

And, of course, that's when I started putting on the weight.
Somebody had to eat those cookies. Wouldn't want the
little lady to think I didn't like her cooking.

(**MRS.C.** *Who you callin' "little"?*)
Nowadays, if you want a deer to fly, you have to train 'em for it special. Strict diet. Low carb. Organic greens. Which there's not a lot of at the North Pole. We had to install a hydroponics garden under the ice cap, and bring in a team of botanists to maintain it. My feed costs went through the roof.

But when life gives you pollution, make pollution-ade. That's what I always say. I went to the factories with the biggest smokestacks and said: "Look, you're putting a lot of toxic ash in the air that future generations are going to have to breathe... But I see you also make lead-based paint. How about you give me a couple hundred gallons of that and we call it even?"

I guess that was my first product placement deal. I started making a lot more of those, because it reduces the number of toys we have to make ourselves. The elves did their best to keep up, but the population was growing fast. And more children means more toys. And more traffic. When we came to town on Christmas Day, all the kids would rush out in the street, and mob the sleigh. It was taking longer and longer to deliver the toys. Couple times I didn't make it home till Boxing Day.

But the thing that coulda killed Christmas was America.
(**SAINT.** *God bless it.*)
You see, when we started out, I talked big about delivering toys to every child in the world, but I was just blowing smoke up Freddik's patoot. We didn't even have charts for half the earth at the time. It would have been impossible to find all those African kids.
(**NIQ.** *And summer-proofing the sleigh is a nightmare.*)
By the late 1700s we were still only bringing Christmas joy to scattered parts of Germany and England, and a handful of Hamlets in Denmark. We weren't even doing a whole country yet.
(**KLAUS.** *Cautious growth.*)

But I'd heard about this new place called the United States, and I thought I'd give it a shot. Small, but manageable. It was technically a country, but sparsely populated. And extremely poor. You didn't even have to bring toys to some of those New England kids. They'd kill for a lump of coal in winter.

I made a couple endorsement deals to distribute locally-grown sorghum, textiles and tobacco to the American children, and we pulled it off! An entire country in one day! A small, poverty-stricken, frontier country, but still. This was big! We were finally on the map.

Then in 1803 the map changed. President Jefferson signed the Louisiana Purchase and the whole thing tripled in size overnight. Now there were kids moving from Boston to Seattle who expected the same service there, that they were getting on the East Coast. Suddenly, I was responsible for an operation that spanned an entire hemisphere.

I admit I was overwhelmed. Even the elves were ready to throw in the towel. Freddik said we should just drop America and keep Christmas a European holiday like God intended. But you can call the Jolly Old Elf a lot of things:

> (**MRS.C.** *Fatso!*)
> (**KRINGLE.** *Tub o' lard!*)
> (**NIQ.** *Acorn smuggler!*)
> (**SAINT.** *Heretic!*)
> (**RED.** *Sugar Freak!*)
> (**KLAUS.** *Lush!*)

But "quitter" isn't one of them. You know my motto: Make pollution-ade.

I called an emergency staff meeting in the main conference room—Elves. Reindeer. Everybody.—And I bolted all the doors. "We are not leaving here," I told them, "Until we figure out how to deliver these toys to those colonists. Now let's hear some ideas. Cuz, frankly, I'm stumped."

That brainstorming session lasted all day. And it was some of the worst ideas I ever heard: Gift certificates. Counting ketchup as a present. Murdering children in their sleep to cut costs! I mean, seriously, the worst ideas.

But as the meeting dragged on into evening, and the sun sank lower in the sky, and the reindeer were starting to smell. The elves realized I was serious about keeping them after hours—Most people don't know this, but elves are deathly afraid of the dark. That's why we hang strings of lights everywhere.

"You can't keep us here all night!" they said. "Yes, I can," I told them.

(**KLAUS.** *Read your contract.*)

"Because *this* old elf does not give up on a child just because he or she is difficult, or hard to please. We are going to find a way to get these toys to those kids, and if we have to work through the night to do it, then so be it: We will work through the night!"

(**RED.** *Work through the night?*)

You could have heard a pin drop.

(**NIQ.** *Why didn't I think of that?*)

It was so simple, it was stupid.

(**SAINT.** *The night* before *Christmas.*)

After that, we went in at night. With the children all snug in their beds, we were in and out in half the time. Less traffic. And we didn't have to waste time chatting up the parents or signing stockings.

(**KRINGLE.** *Or doing laps.*)

Some of the houses were locked, but I'd drop an elf down the chimney and they'd let me in the back door.

That first night just seemed to fly by: Europe was done in a twinkling. Then we raced the sunrise across the Atlantic, swooped in off the Gulf Stream to do the East Coast, then rapid as eagles: Gulf Coast, Midwest, Southwest, and hit the Pacific Rim in time to finish the entire continent by daybreak on the West Coast.

After that, nothing was impossible, and no one ever doubted me again.

Once you've conquered America, the world is your stocking.

SANTA 7 – "Big S"
"Fame Changes Everything"

That was my breakout year.

Before the Century was over, Christmas had become an inter-national holiday.

And I had become a household name.

That's when things got a little freaky:

If you've never been famous, you don't know what it's like. You can't.

Because it's exactly not like anything that happens to ordinary people in every day life.

And I wasn't just well-known. I was *world-renowned*. No small feat in a world where news was spread by steam rail and carrier pigeon.

You try getting that kind of media penetration without a music video.

Or a sex tape on YouTube.

Everywhere I went, I got the velvet rope and the red carpet.

I had the best tables at the finest restaurants. Front row seats. Box seats. Sometimes they'd build boxes, just so I could have a seat.

People I never even heard of were acting like they were my best friends.

And friends I'd known since childhood – were fetching me coffee now.

And *everyone* seems to think your life is their business.

Whether that's your sexuality or your medical history, or the way you do your job.

Kids started writing letters telling me what I had to bring them for Christmas.

Excuse me?

First of all, kid, how did you get this address?

And second, who died and made me God?

You want a pony?

Who the fuck do you think you are?

Santa never got a pony, but you think you deserve one?

And which chimney would you like me to shove it down?

I ought to do that sometime.

Leave a mangled horse carcass bleeding on a stretcher in the living room.

With a big bow around its broken neck.

"Look what Santa brought you!

Oh, and here's a shiny new rifle so you can put it out of its misery."

(**MRS.C.** *Ugh!*)

I started getting paternity suits from people I'd never been with.

Gay-ternity suits from people I'd never been gay with.

Everybody wanted a piece of me. Like a pumpkin pie. Or a wishbone from a turkey.

Because my name was synonymous with Christmas.

Which pissed off the Church, because Christ's name was synonymous with getting your thumb caught in a door.

A bunch of nutjobs in Rome tried to get the Pope to declare a fatwa against me, because I was destroying the institution of Christmas.

Then they realized the institution was pretty fucked up before I came along, so they got me an expedited Sainthood instead—so they could pray directly to me for presents, 'cause they were too cheap to buy a stamp like everyone else.

I wasn't even a person anymore.

I was an icon—a figurehead.

(**NIQ.** *I was also a bobble-head doll.*)

Overnight, I'd gone from being the poor son of a poor cobbler – to the third most powerful force in the universe.

Gravity being first. And, of course, Fame second.

Because Fame changes *everything*.

And you don't expect it to change you, too. But it does.

(**KLAUS.** *That's just physics.*)

You don't mean to be different.

But when valet treatment becomes the norm, you start to think something's wrong when somebody doesn't offer to park your sled.

You start to think: Why is this marching band so much smaller than the ones I'm used to?

And how come the key to this city isn't gold like the last one I got?

You start asking for stupid stuff like bottled water and free-range veal. Gourmet toilet paper, and pre-filtered air—And can we do something about the frequency of this light?

You ask for green M & Ms, not because you want them, but because it's fun to watch the interns scramble.

Soon you're making the elves audition for shit jobs and playing elimination games with the reindeer to see who's still on the team.

You're spending money on expensive manicures, and pedicures, and beardicures. Designer caps and mittens.

This is real fur.

Have you ever seen "pleather"? Check this out:

That's genuine platypus leather.

And the wilder things get, the more normal it seems, until you don't know what "normal" means anymore.

> (**MRS.C.** *Hey, Santa, show us your tits!*)
> (**RED.** *Did you sleep with that reindeer?*)
> (**KLAUS.** *Over here! Big S! Big S!*)
> (**KRINGLE.** *We love you Santa!*)

Do normal people have vibrating massage seats on their toilets? And a chocolate fondue fountain on the dashboard of their sleigh?

Do elves floss their teeth? Or is that what the entourage is for?

Is it normal to secretly videotape your groupies having sex without their knowledge? Or do you get a signed released form first?

Do ordinary people drink thousand dollar bottles of champagne in the hot tub? Or do they get by with three hundred dollar bottles – and Cuban cigars.

And how much cocaine is too much?

And what does it matter what ordinary people do anyway?

I'm fucking Santa Claus.

I'll never be normal again.

I drive a fucking sleigh for Christ's sake.

> (**NIQ.** *And it's a stretch hummer.*)

I dress however I like.

You think I care what anyone else thinks about fashion? I make fashion.

You get it under your tree. And you *like* it.

This year you're gonna be wearing luon. Trust me, you'll love it, it breathes.

You think you can tell me when I've had too much to drink?

Who I should talk to?

What I should get them?

Where I can touch them?

I own fucking Christmas, sugar tits.

I decide what's under the tree!—Hell, I am the tree.

You just say, "thank you"—and mean it!—or next year you shop for your own sex toys.

> (**SAINT.** *Good Lord…*)

You're going to judge me?

I've seen you when you're sleeping.

I know what you do when you're awake.

I know when you've been bad, good, borderline.

I've got a list.

They give me a printout.

You fuck with me, you get coal in your stocking.

Or forget the coal. I'm a fucking Saint.

Fuck with me, I'll send you straight to hell.

> (**J.O.E.** *Uh oh.*)
> (**RED.** *Holy shit…*)

How'd you like to spend the holiday roasting chestnuts over an open lake of fire?

That's right, faggot! Santa will burn your fucking soul!

I will fry you in frankincense!

Then I'll take the smoldering cinder that used to be your

heart – and I'll put it in someone else's socks, just to piss them off!
How ya like them persimmons?! Huh!?!

(**SAINT.** *Okaaay…*)

[*Mrs. Claus and the others come in to restrain him.*]

MRS. CLAUS
"Power Over Rehab"

I think Santa needs a rest.
Thank you for that share, hon, that was endearing.
Let's get you some coffee. Decaf.
No, it's okay, you sit down.
Somebody help him.

All right.
Is there anybody else?
Vilmer, did you want to say something? Then shut up!

My name is Francesca Natalia Claus-Raufvenshemmer.
And I have been clean and sober for 45 minutes.

I run the North Pole Thursday meetings—because the rest
of you are a bunch of pussies. So until someone proves
they're a bigger drunk than me, I'm in charge here.

I started coming—I don't know how long ago—nor do I
care. But I wear the ten-year pin, because it's pretty. And
it's how you know I outrank you. 'Cause, look around,
nobody else even has five.

The pin reminds me of my first day in rehab. Because
that's when I got it.

You see, practically the first thing they tell you when you
walk in the door – is that the first step is admitting you're
powerless over alcohol. Since I have not in my experience
found it to be the case that I am powerless over anything: It
seemed that rehabilitation and I had reached an impasse.

But that also sounded kind of defeatist. So I decided instead that rehab was powerless over me. I promptly had our leader thrown out of the meeting, and awarded myself the ten-year pin for conquering detox.

He wasn't hurt, he's fine.

Now he runs the Monday afternoon meeting for pussies. If you can't handle this meeting, you can come back on Monday to have your hand held and your ego fluffed. Here, we talk straight, shoot from the hip and ask questions later. We don't pull our punches, and afterwards—if you don't piss me off—there's a keg chilling in the back of my pickup for anyone wants a tailgater.

Now, I want to tell this story in honor of our newest court-ordered guest. Without whom, none of us would be here tonight. And by that, I mean: here in this meeting. My husband has driven more people to drink than a Catholic seminary. And I think we all owe him for that. Which, I guess, makes tonight payback.

I had my first drink on our wedding night.

Of course, in those days the drinking age was considerably lower. As was the age of consent. And he's lucky the statute of limitations ran out on a couple of other things that happened that night!

But that's a story for another time.

So count your blessings, Daddy! The only thing keeping you in that red suit and out of an orange one is a couple hundred years of belated women's suffrage. And the fact that I'm a size queen. But you knew that when you abducted me from that orphanage!

Although, in those days, it was called courting.

Fatass over there—but I guess this is supposed to be anonymous, so—my alleged husband—drugged a nun and smuggled me out of the orphan home and back to his father's cobbler shop. Where he'd set up a makeshift rape-room-slash-honeymoon-suite in the tanning shed out back. With a heart-shaped pile of leather remnants for a bed.

Tres romantic.

He clumsily professed his love for me—and anyone who looked like me—and anything with a pulse.

Virgins are adorable, aren't they?

Then, when it was clear that flattery was getting him nowhere. He took out a bottle. Which at first I thought he was going to bludgeon me with. But then he screwed off the cap, and gave me a sip of something he called "tequila". I'd never had anything like it. It was like a cross between a mouthful of donkey urine, and 30ccs of morphine.

(**RED.** *Lightweight.*)

After a couple shots of that, he showed me some bawdy playing cards, and asked me if I'd like to play a game. In hindsight, I should have said, "Yes", because it would have saved me listening to him whine and beg for half an hour, before I ended up agreeing to play strip poker, anyway.

Though in those days, it had the more evocative nickname of "Vicars and Virgins".

I found it to be a very confusing game—as the rules seemed to change every time I had a good hand. Before I knew it, I was sitting in my undergarments on the leather bed, as he stood over me—declared himself the winner—and announced that I was to be penalized.

I think because he liked saying "peen".

Six months later, we exchanged vows. But I wanted to

wear white at the wedding. So I got them to back-date the marriage license to that first "poker night." Making what happened there our holy consummation.

After it was all over, and I was lying there sweaty and exhausted—from the exertion of rolling him off of me—He was lively and quick that night, let me tell you.—I decided to wake him up and ask for more tequila. Because on the whole that had been the least gruesome part of the ordeal.

And I've been schnockered ever since.

Who knows? If the sex had been better that night, I might be next door at the nympho-holics meeting instead. Getting schnockered a few other ways.

[raises a toast]

God bless erectile dysfunction.

[drinks]

Allegedly.

SEVEN SANTAS

RED. I don't have to sit here and stand for this. I am not impotent.

MRS.C. Allegedly.

BIG S. I am Santa Claus. I am the most famous person on the earth.

RED. I'm a fucking saint, for God's sake.

SAINT. (Pardon my French.)

RED. I get laid plenty.

MRS.C. Probably not something you wanna say to a gal without a prenup.

BIG S. I've got women throwin' themselves at me.

KRINGLE. *Young* women.

NIQ. And men.

RED. And transgenders.

KRINGLE. I mean, *young.*

KLAUS. Yes, we get it.

BIG S. They write me letters.

J.O.E. They call me Dear Santa.

KRINGLE. They stand in line for hours just to give me a lap dance.

MRS.C. They're not there to dance.

RED. Yeah, right, they just wiggle cuz they're fidgety.

J.O.E. Do you know what it's like to show up at someone's house on Christmas Eve and find them curled up next to the fireplace in their Santa jammies, sucking their thumb like some obscene sugar plum?

BIG S. Or tucked into bed wearing nothing but a mistletoe t-shirt and Santa panties.

RED. Don't try to tell me "no means no" when she's got my face embroidered on her crotch. And "Ho Ho Ho" spelled out in candy canes across her ass.

MRS.C. What are you doing peeking in their bedrooms?

J.O.E. To see if they're sleeping. I've got to know when they're awake.

MRS.C. That better be all you're knowing. I'm not bailin' you out on no felony.

RED. Jesus Christ, woman! Do I look like a pedophile?

NIQ. (In that outfit?)

RED. I'm a married man, in case you forgot.

MRS.C. Yeah, and I was 14, at the time, in case *you* forgot. So you got a history.

KLAUS. I shouldn't even dignify that.

RED. I was 16, too, you rummy little whore. You keep harpin' on that like it was statutory, people are gonna start to believe you.

MRS.C. You want to bump it up to date rape? You're not much at plea bargaining.

SAINT. (I'm here, aren't I?)

RED. And that was not a date. It was our honeymoon.

NIQ. (And I've got the rugburns to prove it.)

MRS.C. You really are a charmer, Red.

RED. Bitch all you want, but I didn't see you running back to the orphanage the first time we had a big fight.

BIG S. And I threw you out of the house.

KLAUS. And changed the locks.

SAINT. And drove you back to the orphanage.

MRS.C. You know I could never go back to that orphanage.—They're out of olives.

NIQ. Now I know why they call 'em chains of matrimony.

BIG S. Cuz it's like being handcuffed to a radiator?

RED. They ought to call it waterboarding.

KRINGLE. That kinda makes it sound like an Olympic event.

J.O.E. Oh, it's an Olympic event, all right. A good marriage requires strength, endurance, stamina, quick reflexes—

RED. And a mean backhand.

MRS.C. You also might want to look into some performance-enhancing drugs.

RED. You know what else I might want?

MRS.C. What?

RED. Shut up!

NIQ. Sounds like somebody could use couples counseling.

SAINT. I supposed I could do it.

BIG S. I think you need a license for that.

SAINT. I am an ordained minister.

BIG S. I mean to prescribe whatever hallucinogens you're on:

You can't be your own marriage counselor.

SAINT. Do you know anyone more qualified?

KLAUS. (This far north?)

RED. I know a couple bartenders.

SAINT. As a canonized clergyman I have over two thousand years experience dealing with marital crises. ...Well, the church does.

BIG S. Yeah? How's that going?

SAINT. About 40%.

RED. Hey, I like those odds! *[to* MRS.C*]* Y'hear that, honey? There's hope for us yet.

MRS.C. You're funny, sug. Where's my taser?

BIG S. I think she means it.

RED. Shit...

[MRS. CLAUS chases him with a taser.]

J.O.E. Oy. Is it too late to request jail time?

MRS.C. Nah, this is better. This way we both suffer.

J.O.E. Why does anybody have to suffer?

SAINT. Why does anybody have to live?

KRINGLE. *[to* SAINT*]* Why do you do that?

NIQ. You know, if you go up and stand at the North Pole facing south and stare out across the desolation of the ice cap, the whole world starts to look like one giant white prison. There's no walls. And no bars.

MRS.C. (And no piña coladas.)

NIQ. But we're all stuck here. And there's no getting off.

J.O.E. It's a life sentence.

KLAUS. And there's no appeal.

BIG S. (You could even say it blows.)

NIQ. And it really doesn't matter if you serve your time in a cold metal box. Or a tropical island. There's no escape. You're going to die here.

SAINT. "All the world's a cage, and all the men and women merely convicts."

RED. We're all trapped in dead-end jobs, and loveless marriages.

KLAUS. Hounded by creditors—

BIG S. And the press—

SAINT. And nagging doubts—

J.O.E. (I feel like a prisoner in my own body.)

KRINGLE. Burdened by guilt.

KLAUS. Locked into commitments with ironclad contracts—

SAINT. And holy vows—

NIQ. Crazy deadlines—

BIG S. Paparazzi.

KLAUS. But commitment to what, exactly?

RED. It doesn't matter. I said I'd do it, and I keep my word.

KLAUS. But the minute you take responsibility for anything, you're saddled with it.

SAINT. No good deed goes unpunished. You knew that when you took this job.

J.O.E. How am I supposed to get ahead, when my reputation always precedes me?

BIG S. That's the price of fame.

SAINT. The toll of holiness.

NIQ. The curse of genius.

SAINT. Your *genius*? That's your great cross to bear?

NIQ. Aw, fuck off. You're burdened by holiness.

SAINT. Do you know how hard that is—with all the temptation out there—to live up to my own standards?

NIQ. You think that's tough? Try surpassing them.
I'm expected to top myself year after year.
The Easter Bunny can send out the same goddamn eggs, every Passover, but at Christmas, it's always gotta be bigger, better, brighter.

KRINGLE. (Fluffier.)

NIQ. Glitzier, pricier, more moving parts, bigger ram cache.

KLAUS. Easier to use. Harder to find.

NIQ. Dolls gotta blink, gotta talk, gotta pee, gotta giggle and dance.

RED. Dolls gotta do laundry.

KRINGLE. (Fluffier.)

BIG S. And this year we're gonna add another reindeer.

J.O.E. Eight's not enough?

BIG S. Yeah, but this one glows.

RED. And now we're shooting a new Christmas special.

BIG S. This one's a musical!

RED. Can you sing?

BIG S. Can you rap?

RED. Can you fire an AK47?

NIQ. Do you know how hard it is to come up with a new Harry Potter book each year?

MRS.C. You don't write the Harry Potter books.

NIQ. No, but that's what it's like.

J.O.E. How did I end up on this treadmill? I wasn't trying to be famous, or rich.

MRS.C. (Or good-looking, obviously.)

J.O.E. I certainly wasn't trying to be a role model.

BIG S. (Well, there's your first mistake.)

KRINGLE. I just wanted some kids to have persimmons for Christmas.

RED. Complain all you want, man boobs, but I don't see you doin' anything that's gonna fix the problem.

J.O.E. I'm here, aren't I?

RED. Putting a butt in a seat ain't gonna change the world.

MRS.C. (Tell that to my theatre company.)

KLAUS. People don't come here to change. They come here to stay the same.

BIG S. They come here to say: "Look at me, judge! See how hard I'm trying not to be the person you arrested? Now, can you please clear my name and let me get back to what I was doing before you caught me?"

SAINT. (That's not how it works.)

MRS.C. And could the rest of the world please change around me, so I don't have to do anything else? Because this is really all I'm comfortable with.

NIQ. Yeah, I did my part. What's anybody else doing to solve my problems?

SAINT. Excuse me, but some of us _are_ here to change.

[Silence.]

Not me, but some of us.

KRINGLE. I'll change.

[Stands and raises right hand.]

I, Santa Claus, being of sound mind and body—

NIQ. (Body, not so much, but go ahead.)

KRINGLE. —do solemnly swear to make it my New Year's resolution never to drink or touch or even look at alcohol, or drugs, or any kind of mind-or-body-altering controlled substance of any kind. For as long as I live. As God is my witness. *[quickly]* Including Viagra, amen.

RED. You would, you asexual little freak!

KRINGLE. I am not asexual!

RED. You will be when I get done with you.

[RED chases KRINGLE.]

KRINGLE. I'm not afraid of you.

RED. Then stop running.

J.O.E. All right, break it up, you.

SAINT. You're not going to hurt him.

RED. He doesn't know that!

[RED chases KRINGLE.]

KLAUS. *[to MRS. CLAUS]* Aren't you going to do something?

MRS.C. Hell, no, this is why I come to these things.

[She drinks.]

Hit 'im in the sleigh bells!

[RED catches KRINGLE.]

KRINGLE. You're the reason we're here!

RED. I am not an alcoholic!

J.O.E. You're drunk right now.

RED. That's two different things.

KLAUS. What kind of person goes to rehab hung over?

ALL. Everybody.

MRS.C. (You think I want to be sober for this?)

KRINGLE. Let me go!

RED. You take back what you said.

BIG S. Leave him alone before you do something we all regret.

RED. He already has.

KRINGLE. I don't know what you're talking about…

RED. You made a promise you know you can't keep.

MRS.C. (God, this takes me back.)

NIQ. So what if he did?

BIG S. Why do you care?

RED. Because I – unlike some people – am a man of my word.

SAINT. A solemn vow should not be taken lightly.

BIG S. So he's going to hell. What's it matter to you?

RED. You're not taking me with you.

NIQ. No, I think you'll be driving that bus.

RED. Fuck you!

NIQ. I'm not your type.

SAINT. Patience, my son—

RED. And you're not my father.

SAINT. No. I'm you.

RED. You're nothing like me.

KRINGLE. You're wearing the same pants.

RED. I'll kill you!

[RED chases KRINGLE.]

KLAUS. Look, I think he's right. We all ought to take a vow of abstinence.

J.O.E. Oy.

BIG S. That's a deal breaker.

KLAUS. From alcohol, I mean.

RED. No.

KLAUS. We're in this situation because of a drinking problem.

All we have to do is swear off alcohol. Clean slate. Expunge the records. And get back to work. The work is what's important.

NIQ. Spoken like a true workaholic.

BIG S. You get your fix at the office. What's in it for me?

SAINT. Look at you. You're going through withdrawal right now, aren't you?

KLAUS. People are counting on me. Children are counting on me.

KRINGLE. (Children aren't people?)

KLAUS. We've got a job to do.

J.O.E. I hate to say this—

RED. Then shut up.

J.O.E. But he's got a point, you know.

KLAUS. I do?

J.O.E. This whole tragic inconvenience has been a wake up call.

MRS.C. (Then where's my Bloody Mary?)

J.O.E. For the sake of the kids, we've got to stop closing our eyes to the situation, and see this for what it is:

RED. An exercise in co-dependence?

SAINT. A golden opportunity.

J.O.E. We've been given a second chance, if we want it.

NIQ. Let's make golden opportunit-ade!

KRINGLE. (Watersports! Yay!)

J.O.E. It's time to stop running from the problem, and have the courage to face up to our own weaknesses.

RED. Maybe I don't have weaknesses.

BIG S. Or maybe you just don't have the guts to admit it.

RED. I've got guts enough for ten guys.

KLAUS. (From India. Three from America.)

RED. I don't have a drinking problem.

NIQ. No, but the rest of us have a problem. And it's *your* drinking.

RED. How is my drinking your problem?

J.O.E. Because I can't talk to a child at the mall without worrying about how my breath mints are holding up.

KRINGLE. They won't sit on my lap if I smell like their uncle.

BIG S. I'm tired of being called "Party Claus" in all the tabloids.

KLAUS. And we're losing 35 sick days a year to hangover and related ailments.

RED. I told you to put "exhaustion".

SAINT. I'm sick of doing mea culpas for things I barely remember.

NIQ. And think of your future: Liver damage will not go with that outfit.

RED. So I'm killing myself. At least I'm not hurting anyone.

MRS.C. You're hurting me, Red.

RED. Aw shut up. You're a lush yourself. Shouldn't there be a rule against alcoholics speaking at an intervention?

SAINT. Then maybe you should shut up and listen.

RED. You act like I'm the only one here with a problem.

NIQ. No, you're the only one who *is* a problem.

RED. My consumption is exactly commensurate for a man of my proportionate girth and stature.

MRS.C. (You're slurring your vocabulary, hon.)

RED. Or it would be if it weren't for you!

SAINT. Me?

> *[RED grabs SAINT NICK's flask.]*

RED. *This* is what puts me over the legal limit.

SAINT. My drinking is strictly sacramental.

RED. And you. Martini for lunch.

BIG S. (So I'm social.)

RED. Wine with dinner.

KRINGLE. (The tannins are good for you.)

RED. A toddy before bed.

J.O.E. (Just to relax me.)

RED. And *you.*

KLAUS. I have been clean and sober for over a generation.

RED. Yeah, you stopped having a drinking problem when cocaine stopped coming in 12oz bottles.

KLAUS. That was for medicinal purposes!

BIG S. What? For your glaucoma?

KLAUS. I would not need prescription-strength stimulants if the most massive logistical achievement in the known universe was not complicated by this endless circus of hedonistic pursuits.

SAINT. A lifelong dedication to the holiest of holidays is not hedonistic.

MRS.C. I'll drink to that! Lifelong holidays!

KLAUS. I have this completely under control. I am still perfectly capable of performing my job. And that of ten other people.

NIQ. And you can quit any time?

KLAUS. Of course, I can.

NIQ. I mean the job.

KLAUS. What? And leave it to the elves? They can't even floss right!

MRS.C. (You're not holding 'em right.)

KLAUS. We are on a schedule here. Certain things have to be done at certain times with certain colors of ribbon. There's no margin for error.

NIQ. Then work-related stress is just what the doctor ordered.

KLAUS. This is a huge responsibility you're asking me to shirk.

SAINT. Nobody asked you to spend your whole life on it either, did they?

KLAUS. Well—

BIG S. *[interrupting]* No, but they sure went crazy for it when I did:

"Santa's comin' to town! Break out the cookies and milk."

KRINGLE. ("Ho ho ho!")

RED. Wassail and incense!

BIG S. Eggnog and rum!

KRINGLE. ("Hi, kids!")

RED. Cider and schnapps!

KRINGLE. ("Wait a minute, this isn't incense.")

BIG S. That's okay Santa, buddy, have another hit.

RED. Just keep the toys coming. And we'll hook you up.

BIG S. You like elves? We got elves.

RED. Leprechauns?

BIG S. Altar boys?

RED. You're ordained, right? It's not a sin if you're willing to forgive yourself.

SAINT. That's not how it works.

KRINGLE. ("Maybe just a small one.")

BIG S. You want some peppermint poppers?

KRINGLE. ("Yay!")

RED. How 'bout a pound of 'mistletoe'?

KRINGLE. ("Okay.")

BIG S. Here, I'll roll it for you.

KRINGLE. ("Thanks.")

RED. You need a light?

KRINGLE. ("This is nice.")

J.O.E. Are you saying that was not mistletoe I smoked at the Christmas party?

ALL. *[disbelief]* Oh, come on!

BIG S. Did it smell like mistletoe?

J.O.E. How would I know? I am just a humble boot maker from a tiny village.

BIG S. In a tiny valley, through a tiny mountain range, across a tiny continent on a little bitty tiny planet— which you practically own—but you had no idea this kind of stuff goes on there.

KLAUS. Don't be a prude. We all smoked it.

SAINT. Even I smoked it. God'll forgive me.

KRINGLE. I did, too.

NIQ. Oh, I smoked it.

RED. Me, too.

NIQ. But I didn't inhale.

BIG S. Yeah—What?

SAINT. You're kidding, right?

NIQ. What?

RED. You are not the one I expected to say that.

BIG S. You expect us to believe you never fired up a Yule log?

NIQ. Believe what you want, it's a free ice cap.

J.O.E. Aren't you the guy who wants to legalize it? And sell it to school children? On the playground?

KLAUS. There's a lot of money in that, y'know.

NIQ. I have never said anything remotely like that.

J.O.E. No, but it kinda goes without saying.

NIQ. Why does everyone equate legalization with utilization?

RED. *[sarcastic]* Yeah, I dunno. That's a stretch.

NIQ. Just because I'm open to new ideas, doesn't mean I have to try every single one of them.

RED. Why not? If you don't have a problem with it?

NIQ. Because that would make me self-destructive: Being tolerant of others doesn't mean I have to make all the same mistakes. Some experiences are better second hand, frankly.

RED. Like what?

NIQ. Like you don't have to go through childbirth to know it looks awful painful. You don't have to kill someone with your bare hands to know that war is an idiotic idea. And you don't have to drop acid to know you like your reality straight up. No olive. No twist.

MRS.C. (Oo! Make mine a double!)

BIG S. Yeah, but still. Why are you being so defensive?

KRINGLE. Yeah, what do you care what we think?

NIQ. I care because you're stereotyping me. And yourself, and everyone else. You expect the whole world to fall neatly into categories, when you've got a list right there in your pocket that tells you that no two kids are alike. Little Michael Piper plays football, but he likes dolls.

MRS.C. (Because he's gay.)

NIQ. Frannie Raufvenshemmer likes sex, but she hates her husband.

RED. (Cuz she's a whore.)

NIQ. Jeannie Rancini loves animals, but she's afraid of reindeer.

KRINGLE. (She's gay *and* a whore. This is fun.)

SAINT. (Stop it.)

NIQ. You act like there are just two types of snowflakes— the round ones and the square ones—and everyone is either one or the other, or they're not a snowflake!!

BIG S. Are you high?

NIQ. No! That's the point. You don't have to be high to think outside the box.

MRS.C. He's high.

NIQ. I'm high on life. I'm high on ideas and creativity.

RED. Oh, I see what the problem is: You're high on who you are.

NIQ. Yes, I am!

RED. You like yourself.

NIQ. Yes, I do.

RED. And if you were high on something else—it might mean it wasn't you you liked, after all.

NIQ. That's not what I said—

BIG S. How brilliant can you be if all your talent comes from inside a pill bottle?

SAINT. Or a pack of something anyone can buy on a street corner?

NIQ. I am not on anything. And these are ordinary cigarettes.

SAINT. Oh, so you're just wildly creative.

NIQ. And mildly caffeinated. But that's it.

J.O.E. Then maybe it's the caffeine that's doing it.

NIQ. No, the coffee just makes me edgy.

BIG S. And acid makes me quirky.

RED. And the alcohol makes me complex.

KRINGLE. (Ecstasy makes me do things in my pants.)

KLAUS. With the right combination of chemicals, you don't need to have a personality at all.

BIG S. So what is it you're *not* on, again? Wheatgrass?

NIQ. I do not have a problem.

RED. Nobody said it was a problem.

NIQ. Then why are we talking about it?

BIG S. Because you don't seem to want to.

KLAUS. Supply and demand. The less you say, the more interesting you become.

BIG S. The more you deny it, the more we want the truth. Otherwise, it's: "Y'know, I think he might be on methamphetamines..."

SAINT. "He hasn't been eating lately."

RED. "I heard it was heroin."

KRINGLE. "Do you think he looks gay in that outfit?"

J.O.E. "You know, I did notice one of the gerbils was missing."

KLAUS. "Have you seen his pictures? They're all over the internet."

MRS.C. "They're kinda blurry, but I guess it could be him..."

NIQ. All right!!

[Beat.]

...I have a drinking problem.

BIG S. You see? Now that's boring.

NIQ. I do, I have a drinking problem.

ALL. Boring!

NIQ. I'm an alcoholic.

RED. *[overlapping]* Blah blah blah...

KLAUS. *[overlapping]* Yeah yeah yeah...

J.O.E. *[overlapping]* HO HO HO!

KRINGLE. *[overlapping]* Yadda yadda yada...

BIG S. *[overlapping]* Been there, done that.

NIQ. No, it's true, I admit it. I've got a beer bong in the back of the toyshop and all winter long I'm slamming boilermakers and peppermint cosmopolitans, just waitin' for Christmas to be over.

KLAUS. (Whatever.)

NIQ. I've got a thermos of hot cocoa and grain alcohol in the glove compartment, cuz it's the only way to keep warm in that sleigh.

ALL. (*Yaaawn...*)

NIQ. I am an alcoholic.

KRINGLE. (Golf clap.)

SAINT. Congratulations. You did the right thing.

MRS.C. Yeah, I think we got a pin for that.

NIQ. Thank you, thank you. I'm an alcoholic.

RED. What the hell, I am, too.

SAINT. My name is Father Christmas, and I'm an alcoholic.

BIG S. Me, too.

J.O.E. I am an alcoholic.

KRINGLE. So am I.

NIQ. You're right, that was very therapeutic.

KLAUS. I think I might have a drinking problem.

MRS.C. (That makes two of us.)

KRINGLE. Isn't it wonderful that we can all come here and have the same problem together, like one big happy family?

SAINT. Yeah, but drinking's not your problem.

KRINGLE. ...It's not?

RED. No, it's kids.

J.O.E. Kids?

SAINT. Yes, kids.

J.O.E. How could children possibly be a problem?

KLAUS. *[interrupting]* How can they not?

Kids! Always whining.

Always wheedling.

Always wanting.

Wanting more.

And when you give it to 'em?

They get worse!

Satisfying a child doesn't make them stop wanting. It makes them louder.

They're insatiable.

BIG S. I can't go to a strip mall without I get a mob of kids lined up in the street blocking traffic. Trying to be the first to see Santa Claus. It doesn't matter that every kid on the planet gets a visit from Saint Nick. They all want to be first in line.

RED. We used to have this toy: The GI Joe.

And all the kids had one.

But they didn't want the same one.

They want the *best* one.

They wanted their Joe to be better than the Joe next door.

KLAUS. So we added a blond-haired Joe and a redhead Joe.

NIQ. And Joe in the Navy and Joe in the Marines.

BIG S. And Malibu Barbie. And gay fashion Ken.

NIQ. And personalized Cabbage Patch Kids, so each and every one of them could have a toy that was completely different and definitively better than every other kid on earth.

KLAUS. So they could all have the only toy of its kind in the whole wide world. …Just like everybody else.

SAINT. How did Christmas get to be the most selfish day of the year?

J.O.E. It brings out the best and the worst in kids.

RED. And then it gives the worst a BB gun so it can shoot out the other one's eye.

J.O.E. You know what you got for Christmas when I was little? A pair of socks. Nice warm pair of winter socks. And that was it. And you were happy to have 'em.

RED. Now that's not good enough. Nowadays that's the cruelest thing you can give a child is socks.

J.O.E. I don't have to bring coal anymore. A kid can tell how naughty they've been just by how many pair of socks are under the tree.

RED. You've been really bad you get underwear.

KRINGLE. (That was my idea.)

SAINT. So what do you want to do? Abstain from children?

NIQ. Y'know, that's not as crazy as it sounds.

RED. Oh, good. Cuz it sounds completely insane. And I've already been in one straight jacket tonight.

NIQ. Hear me out: We convert Christmas to an adults-only holiday. *[to KLAUS]* You said yourself grownups are where the money is.

BIG S. (Are we talking "drinking-age" adult? Or "cock rings and vibrators" adult?)

RED. (Wait, what's the difference?)

KLAUS. I like it. We skip the kids, go straight for their parents' pocket books. Cut out the middle man.

SAINT. We are *not* going to do that.

NIQ. Why not? It's brilliant!

SAINT. Because I forbid it.

RED. Who died and made you Pope?

SAINT. I'm not the Pope, I'm a Saint.

KLAUS. So, being a Saint means you're the boss?

NIQ. I thought it just made you infallible.

SAINT. No *that's* the Pope.

RED. So what's Sainthood get you?

BIG S. A nifty hat, for one.

SAINT. It means I know right from wrong.

BIG S. So you're not infallible, you just don't do anything wrong.

SAINT. Not that I recall.

MRS.C. (What about our wedding night?)

RED. (You know I was drunk for that.)

NIQ. If you don't make mistakes, then why are we here?

SAINT. Mistakes were made. But that was not my fault.

BIG S. Wasn't it? Cuz I remember them pulling your prints off that sleigh.

SAINT. That girl should not have been there.

MRS.C. Sure, blame the victim. It's time she took responsibility for something.

KLAUS. And why not? We're all partially to blame for

everything. Ask any insurance company.

NIQ. So getting run over was her idea? That's brilliant!

SAINT. Blame whoever you want. *[to* **BIG S***]* But if you'd been going slower...

BIG S. *[to* **J.O.E***]* If you were watching where you were going...

J.O.E. *[to* **RED***]* If you hadn't been drinking...

RED. I wasn't drinking. I never drink in the sleigh.

J.O.E. Then why are we here?

RED. Don't ask me. I was passed out at the time.

[Uncomfortable pause.]

KRINGLE. If drinking's not my problem, why are we here?

MRS.C. Yes, why are you here?   Don't tell me I've got a keg chilling outside for nothing. Cuz if I'm the only one having any... Then I better get started.

BIG S. Well? Are you going to tell her, Mr. Cannot-Tell-A-Lie?

SAINT. That's George Washington.

BIG S. Right, you're Mr. Infallible.

SAINT. And that's the Pope, again.

BIG S. So, what was your deal, then?

SAINT. I'm a Saint. I do the right thing.

BIG S. And...?

SAINT. And the truth is not always what's best.

BIG S. So you can be a Saint and still be a liar?

RED. I think it's one of the requirements.

NIQ. Yeah, it was right on the application.

KRINGLE. What about "Thou shalt not lie"?

SAINT. Actually, that's not in the Bible. Look it up.

BIG S. So lie to her then. Cuz I'd love to hear this story.

NIQ. Yeah! Tell us what happened.

SAINT. No.

NIQ. It's good for the soul, you know—confession.

BIG S. And feel free to embellish.

NIQ. Cuz that's good for the other parts.

SAINT. Well—

KLAUS. I'll tell you what happened.

BIG S. Wasn't talking to you.

KLAUS. Three words…

NIQ. "I'm a dweeb"?

KLAUS. Supply and demand.

BIG S. Oh, shut up.

KLAUS. That's why we're here. It's barter and trade.
They make you an offer. You make a counter.
They meet you half way. You sign a confession.

NIQ. (Supply-side moral relativism.)

KLAUS. How do you get a deer to fly? How do you get an elf
to move to the arctic and build 300 million toys? How
do you get Christians all over the world to celebrate
the birth of someone they'd hogtie to the back of their
pickup truck and drag to death if they ever met him in
person? You just give them a good enough reason.

MRS.C. (Supply and demand.)

KLAUS. You want something. They want something. Then
there's a negotiation: How good is your case? How reli-
able are your witnesses? What am I willing to plead to?
And somewhere between life imprisonment and time
served you come to an agreement.

MRS.C. (A plea bargain.)

NIQ. And if you know somebody, that always helps.

BIG S. And I know everybody: "Good morning, Judge!"

NIQ. "Sorry to wake you."

BIG S. "How's the family?"

NIQ. "Little Nelly. Little Terrence. Little Shelly. Little
Mike."

BIG S. "And how about your nieces and nephews?"

NIQ. "Would you like me to name them off? Cuz I got a
list."

BIG S. "Want me to tell you where they live?"

MRS.C. Aw, Red, you didn't threaten a judge?

RED. No, *he* did. *[points at SAINT NICHOLAS]*

BIG S. Your Honor! Do you really want to go home to your
kids tonight, and tell them who you locked up at work
today?

NIQ. Cuz they're gonna find out on Christmas morning
anyway.

BIG S. When your whole family's gathered around an empty tree. Asking *you* what happened to Santa Claus.

NIQ. "What happened to Christmas?"

BIG S. "What happened to Santa?"

NIQ. You don't want that on your conscience, do you?

KLAUS. So how does reckless endangerment sound?

BIG S. Or how about driving under the influence?

KLAUS. That's better. Happens to the best of us.

BIG S. Why, some of our finest citizens are guilty of that.

KLAUS. Driving under the influence. Perfectly respectable.

NIQ. But under the influence of what? Lithium, cocaine and Viagra? Cuz that's what they're gonna find in your system.

BIG S. Hey! How about alcohol?

KLAUS. Sure. There's nothing wrong with alcohol that a little detox can't clear up.

KRINGLE. Thou shalt not lie.

SAINT. That's not in the Bible.

BIG S. Oh, but I've got the circumstantial evidence right here in the boot flask Mrs. Claus gave me for our anniversary. I must have been reaching down to grab it when it happened.

MRS.C. What happened?

KLAUS. *[ignoring her]* Sold! One count of DUI! Guilty as charged!

BIG S. Sentenced to six months of structured self-pity. Case dismissed.

MRS.C. You never drink in that sleigh.

RED. Hell, no.

KLAUS. You know what my premiums would be like?

J.O.E. I pled down... To a lesser offense.

MRS.C. What were they supposed to charge you with?

SAINT. You don't want to know.

J.O.E. It doesn't matter now.

MRS.C. Red? You never lie to me.

RED. There was an accident...

KRINGLE. There was a little girl named Jeannie...

RED. She fell under the sleigh...

NIQ. She died.

MRS.C. Oh...

SAINT. It was nobody's fault.

J.O.E. It was my fault.

KLAUS. It was her fault.

KRINGLE. She was very naughty.

KLAUS. Fooling around in traffic. What was she doing outside at night? In winter. In her pajamas.

RED. White pajamas. You could barely see her against the snow.

KRINGLE. Why did she go outside?

J.O.E. Where were the parents? That's what I want to know. What was she doing in the street?

NIQ. She was running. On ice.

BIG S. On icy asphalt.

NIQ. Running from the sleigh.

J.O.E. I tried to get her to stop.

SAINT. You should have let her go.

J.O.E. I'm not giving up on this child.

NIQ. I was trying to save her when—

RED. She slipped on the ice.

BIG S. She fell under the deer.

J.O.E. Dasher.

Dancer.

Prancer.

Vixen.

Comet.

Cupid.

Donner.

Blitzen.

They'll never forgive themselves.

RED. I'll never forgive myself.

MRS.C. What was she running from?

KRINGLE. She was scared of the deer.

J.O.E. Children aren't afraid of reindeer.

RED. She was afraid of *you.*

KRINGLE. Me? I love children.

SAINT. We all love children.

BIG S. Who doesn't love children?

J.O.E. Some people shouldn't love children.

KRINGLE. I would never harm a child. Or hurt a child. Or frighten them.

NIQ. Sometimes they get frightened anyway. Sometimes they cry for no reason.

KRINGLE. But I don't make them cry.

KLAUS. I love children.

KRINGLE. I think about them all the time.

KLAUS. All day, every day.

KRINGLE. It's them. It's their fault. It's the kids.

KLAUS. Half the time, they're already bawling when you put them on your lap.

KRINGLE. But I know how to make them stop. A candy cane or a lollipop. Or a tickle in the right place, and their tears go away. And they smile. They smile like all tomorrow.

J.O.E. Jeannie was my favorite. I'm not supposed to have favorites, I suppose. But Jeannie was such a special little girl.

KRINGLE. How her eyes twinkled…

J.O.E. Nose like a cherry.

KRINGLE. She had a smile like warm winter snow. Her laughter makes your whole world melt.

MRS.C. Oh, Kris…

KRINGLE. But I never touched her.

MRS.C. You put her on your lap.

KRINGLE. That's different. It's traditional.

BIG S. Yeah, it sounds real platonic.

KRINGLE. We're just friends.

RED. She was eight.

NIQ. She was tiny.

KRINGLE. All of my friends are tiny.

SAINT. I know how this looks—

KRINGLE. She's just a friend. No matter what you think. No matter what they're saying.

KLAUS. I'm not saying anything.

KRINGLE. Ask her.

BIG S. We can't ask her.

KRINGLE. Oh… Right.

J.O.E. I am very sorry about what happened. But I did nothing wrong.

MRS.C. Then why are you sorry?

J.O.E. If she misunderstood—

KRINGLE. If she took something the wrong way—

J.O.E. She should have asked.

KRINGLE. I would never—

J.O.E. She should not have run away like that.

KRINGLE. It isn't safe. Outside at night. In the snow.

J.O.E. I had to go after her. She could have gotten hurt.

SAINT. She did get hurt.

BIG S. She was screaming. She could have woke the whole neighborhood. She would have ruined Christmas for everyone.

J.O.E. I told her to stop.

KRINGLE. She's very fast for a girl her size.

J.O.E. I'm getting too old to be chasing teenagers around in the snow.

MRS.C. She was eight.

J.O.E. Why didn't I just let her go?

KRINGLE. She'll be fine in the morning. It's just a tantrum.

NIQ. No, I can fix this. The sleigh is parked right there. She can't outrun a sleigh.

RED. Not the way I drive.

SAINT. (Like dry leaves before the wild hurricane.)

NIQ. I caught up to her.

J.O.E. Jeannie, no.

BIG S. She screamed even louder.

KRINGLE. Running and screaming.

NIQ. Okay, here's the plan: I'm going to pull alongside her. Hand me that big candy cane.

RED. You've seen too many movies.

NIQ. You had too many beers.

J.O.E. We swerved.

MRS.C. You hit her?

RED. I bumped her. Maybe.

KLAUS. She slipped. On the ice.

BIG S. She fell.

KRINGLE. No, Jeannie!

J.O.E. No, Dasher!

KLAUS. No, Prancer and Vixen!

BIG S. Comet, Cupid, no!

SAINT. Prancer!

NIQ. Jeannie, no!!

RED. ...Donner and Blitzen.

[Silence.]

NIQ. She was lying there. Tangled in their hooves. Mangled in the snow. Like a broken angel.

KRINGLE. Why do we put the fragilest ornaments at the top of the tree? It's so much farther to fall.

J.O.E. If she had just listened me...

KRINGLE. I would never intentionally harm a child.

J.O.E. That's not who I am.

MRS.C. (Yeah, there's a lotta that goin' around.)

NIQ. There was nothing I could do. She wouldn't have survived.

MRS.C. What did you do?

KRINGLE. I tried to help her.

J.O.E. She was in so much pain.

NIQ. I did what I had to.

KRINGLE. I stopped her crying.

[Silence.]

RED. *[shaking his head]* I swore I would never drink in that sleigh.

MRS.C. You make me sick. And not in a wine before beer kind of way.

J.O.E. What? You can't possibly think that I—

BIG S. *[interrupting]* You see? I told you this would happen! I knew no one would believe me.

SAINT. Oh, why wouldn't they believe you? You're Santa Claus!

BIG S. Because people want to believe the worst. They revel in it! They've been waiting for years for something like this: A scandal that'll bring down Santa Claus. Now I'll never hear the end of it.

MRS.C. It's not always about you.

BIG S. I don't see anybody else on trial here.

KLAUS. No one's on trial. No one's trying to bring down Santa. We just have to get our story straight.

RED. I'm not lying for you.

NIQ. It's not a lie if everyone believes it. Right, Nick?

SAINT. That's not how it works.

NIQ. It's not?

KLAUS. We have to stop talking about this. Can we please change the subject? We don't know what she was running from.

KRINGLE. I didn't know she was afraid of deer.

MRS.C. She wasn't running from the deer.

RED. You weren't there.

MRS.C. I posted bail for you, remember?

RED. Three hours later. Who knows what I said after three hours of interrogation.

SAINT. Without a lawyer, I might add.

KLAUS. I was confused. I was babbling.

SAINT. That confession will never hold up.

KLAUS. It's a misunderstanding, that's all.

SAINT. We'll get it suppressed. This isn't a problem.

MRS.C. Nicholas!

SAINT. What?

MRS.C. I know what happened.

RED. You weren't there.

MRS.C. They called me from the police station.

KLAUS. (You gave them her number?)

NIQ. (I'm allowed one phone call.)

MRS.C. They asked me to bring an extra pair of pants. They told me, when they arrested you, you weren't wearing any.

KRINGLE. I— I must have lost them.

SAINT. A lot was going on that night.

KLAUS. It was very confusing. You must be confused. I know I'm confused.

KRINGLE. It was a cold night—I probably—

KLAUS. Took 'em off to warm them by the fire! Am I still talking? I gotta stop talking.

MRS.C. She was a little girl.

RED. Frannie, this was not my fault.

MRS.C. I want to forgive you… But I can't.

RED. Why not?

MRS.C. Because you haven't apologized!

RED. I haven't done anything!!

[MRS. CLAUS slaps RED.]

KLAUS. Ow!

KRINGLE. *[feels it, too]* Oh.

BIG S. You did not—

SAINT. Turn the other cheek, turn the other cheek—

MRS.C. You're a menace.

[SANTA suddenly lunges at her, grabs her by the throat.]

RED. That's not how the District Attorney saw it. He practically gave me a medal. He asked me for an autograph! I didn't even get a slap on the wrist. I'm Santa Claus! Nothing can touch me.

MRS.C. I can touch you.

RED. Don't let those tae bo classes go to your head, sister. You're not in my weight class.

MRS.C. I want a divorce.

SAINT. What? No.

BIG S. Now, hold on a minute…

RED. You what?

MRS.C. I …want…a divorce.

KLAUS. She's kidding, right?

NIQ. I think she means it this time.

SAINT. We shouldn't rush into this…

MRS.C. Why not? We rushed into the marryin' part.

RED. You can't divorce me.

BIG S. You can't. How would that look?

RED. You're Catholic, and I'm a Saint.

BIG S. Think about what you're saying. We need this marriage.

MRS.C. You need this marriage. I need a six-pack.

RED. You'll be back.

BIG S. 'Cesca, baby…

RED. And you'll bring me a pack of smokes, if you know what's good for you!

BIG S. Wait! …I don't want you to go. You're all I have left. After all that's happened—Everything we've been through…

The tabloids'll tear us apart.

MRS.C. That's the best you can do?

BIG S. What to you want from me?!

MRS.C. I don't even know you anymore.

BIG S. WHY NOT?! I'm in all the papers!!

MRS.C. You're a monster.

RED. I'm Christmas.

MRS.C. Well, now you're half of Christmas. I'm taking Dasher, Prancer, Cupid, and the house. You can keep the rest.

[Pause.]

RED. HO HO HO.

J.O.E. HO HO HO HO HO.

RED. What are you going to do with half a reindeer team? They're nothing without me.

KLAUS. HO HO HO.

SAINT. I'm Santa Claus.

J.O.E. HO HO HO HO.

MRS.C. Somebody has to hold you accountable.

RED. Yeah, but they can't! Because you all want to reward me and cuddle me at the same time.

MRS.C. The Santa I know would never do this.

BIG S. But the Santa you saw on Court TV? He's an asshole who had it coming.

J.O.E. I'm sorry, little girl... But you don't get to make that choice.

BIG S. You can't dissect me, and punish just the bad parts.

J.O.E. Not when the good parts bring Christmas joy into your home.

NIQ. I'm not a bunch of cartoony little caricatures that you can love this one, and hate that one, and love to hate the other one.

"Oh, we like this part, but that part isn't him. And this part is just the booze talking."

RED. I'm one person.

With all the flaws and foibles.

Just like all of you.

No better and no worse.

Well, maybe a little bit better, because I'm Christmas.

J.O.E. All of it. The hot cocoa and the cold fruitcake.

The family quarrels and the stuff in the stockings.

The pair of socks you didn't want, and the nanoPod you do.

It's all part of the same package.

BIG S. And if I stumble now and then. You're gonna keep picking me up and dusting me off. Because nobody likes to see Santa face down in the snow.

KRINGLE. You'll keep looking the other way, because looking right at me means you might see who I really am.

SAINT. And you need the myth of me more than I do.

KLAUS. Supply and demand.

RED. You really think I'm the villain in all this?

I never told you what the old orchard owner made me do for those persimmons.

KLAUS. You think a crappy boot made of leather scraps gets you fresh produce in the middle of winter? That came from his personal stock. You don't get that kind of service working hard and being a good boy.

NIQ. They don't give you a bushel of persimmons because you went to church every Sunday and got down on your knees and prayed for 'em.

KLAUS. But while you're down on your knees there is something you can do.

KRINGLE. Every year, till my father passed away, I was a good boy all year long. And then on Christmas Eve I was naughty for a few minutes—And my father got persimmons for Christmas.

J.O.E. And after he died, I never wanted to see another persimmon as long as I lived.

KRINGLE. That's why we don't give them out at Christmas.

Because I can't stand the smell of them.

MRS.C. Oh, Kris...

RED. And now who's the bad guy? It's hard to pick a side when the story changes with every new chapter.

NIQ. If you're smart, you get to a happy part, and throw the rest of the book in the fireplace:

"O little town of Bethlehem—" The end.

Close the book and walk away.

Cuz you don't want to know what happens after that:

SAINT. The crucifixion and the resurrection. And the inquisition, and the final solution, and the ground invasion.

KLAUS. Declare victory and get out. That's the best strategy. Try to remember Christmas for the good things it brings. And forget all the rest.

MRS.C. I keep dreaming of a white Christmas. But the ones I wake up to are always nightmare shades of gray.

SAINT. That's the dirty secret of the holiday: Once a year, we celebrate the birth of a really terrific guy, who did a lot of really terrific things. But making the world a better place was not one of them. He'd tell you that himself.

J.O.E. No, he left that to me.

Peace on earth. Good will toward men.

That's my job.

RED. I make the world a better place.

Once a year, every year.

Whether it needs it or not.

And there's not a goddamn one of you can say the same.

KLAUS. Sure, I made mistakes.

NIQ. We all make mistakes.

SAINT. (Well, not me. Not officially.)

RED. (Shut up.)

KLAUS. But you don't really care about that.

BIG S. You don't care what I did, or how my recovery's going.

KLAUS. You care about Christmas.

BIG S. All the letters I get: Nobody says, "Dear Santa, How have you been? How was your summer?"

They all say the same thing:

KLAUS. "Give me this. Give me that."

BIG S. Gimme.

NIQ. Gimme.

J.O.E. Gimme.

SAINT. Gimme!

RED. Gimme!

KRINGLE. Gimme!

BIG S. That little girl? You don't even know her.

RED. When you leave here tonight, you won't even remember her name.

BIG S. But you'll remember me.

Because you remember Christmas.

J.O.E. And you remember one Christmas in particular.

And one present more than all the rest.

You know the one.

You thought I forgot.

But I still remember it like it was yesterday.

RED. What was it, a bicycle? Or a doll? I don't recall.

But *you* do.

J.O.E. You'll never forget that gift.

NIQ. You wanted it so bad, you had to tell me about it in October. Your eyes lit up like Bethlehem stars.

KLAUS. You put it at the top of your list, and underlined it. And circled it, and highlighted it, and put a smiley face next to it.

NIQ. Anything to take your mind off the fact that you knew in your heart that you weren't going to get it.

KLAUS. You knew your parents couldn't afford it.

Every time you mentioned it, they grumbled about how it was too dangerous, or too expensive. Or maybe you just didn't deserve it: Trying not to get your hopes up.

NIQ. So you stopped mentioning it. And eventually, you stopped hoping.

KLAUS. You tried to convince yourself that not getting a present that you didn't really need anyway wasn't the worst thing in the world.

NIQ. Even though it felt like it at the time.

J.O.E. That was the year you started to stop believing.

I felt so bad for you.

So young to be understanding the world for the first time.

SAINT. And then something happened...

Somewhere between Thanksgiving and New Year's,

You stopped thinking about Christmas.

You stopped thinking about yourself.

And started thinking about…

Children in other countries.

And other parts of town.

You thought about tsunami victims and hurricanes.

BIG S. That was the year you saved up some of your lunch money and donated it to UNICEF. And even offered to help your sister with her homework.

J.O.E. (You were so good.)

SAINT. (I was so proud of you.)

RED. And when Christmas rolled around,

You'd almost forgot it was coming.

Your parents had to call you twice to get you out of bed.

You trudged into the room with the tree that had stopped shining as brightly as it used to.

KRINGLE. And there it was.

Just like I promised you.

BIG S. The gift you knew you'd never get. Big as day.

SAINT. Big as Christmas Day.

NIQ. Your whole face lit up. You didn't even have to take the ribbons off to know what it was.

BIG S. You ran over and hugged it so tight. I thought you were going to break something.

KRINGLE. You were trembling, you were so happy, sobbing and laughing at the same time. And you had such a smile.

J.O.E. Children are beautiful when they smile. And that morning. You were the most beautiful child on earth.

KLAUS. The perfect gift.

RED. The perfect day.

KRINGLE. I picked that out for you. You remember?

BIG S. I'll never forget.

J.O.E. That's how I always think of Christmas.

That Christmas—That moment. Just the two of us.

NIQ. And every year, we try to recapture it again:

RED. The nip in the air—

SAINT. The song that was playing—

NIQ. Catching snowflakes on your tongue—

J.O.E. The smell of nutmeg—

KLAUS. The lights on the tree have to be just right.

BIG S. I would give anything in the world to see you smile like that again.

KRINGLE. Because if we could just go back to that.

Nothing else would matter.

SAINT. Nothing we've done before or since.

MRS.C. There's a song we sing every year

About putting the past behind us.

We sing it every year,

Because it's the only way we can make it through the next one.

SAINT. The only way to get to the next December 25th is forget all the July 3rds, and September 11ths, and April 15ths that come between. And keep your eye on that star.

KLAUS. That one day that makes up for everything else.

NIQ. Christmas Day.

RED. Our day.

J.O.E. My day to you.

KRINGLE. Merry Christmas, little one.

KLAUS. Merry Christmas to all.

BIG S. And to all a good night.

SAINT. Santa loves you.

NIQ. More than you will ever know.

RED. And he always will.

J.O.E. Ho Ho Ho!

MRS.C. Mazel tov!!

[BLACKOUT]